ON THE FARM, AT THE MARKET

G. BRIAN KARAS

Christy Ottaviano Books

HENRY HOLT AND COMPANY · NEW YORK

I wish to thank Ken Migliorelli of Migliorelli Farm, Gary Wiltbank of Wiltbank Farm, and Rory Chase and Peter Destler at the Amazing Real Live Food Company. The time they afforded me and their helpful explanation of their trade gave me a more complete understanding of how food is grown, made, packed, and sold.

Henry Holt and Company, LLC, *Publishers since 1866*
175 Fifth Avenue, New York, New York 10010
mackids.com

Henry Holt® is a registered trademark of Henry Holt and Company, LLC.
Copyright © 2016 by G. Brian Karas

Library of Congress Cataloging-in-Publication Data
Karas, G. Brian, author, illustrator.
On the farm, at the market / G. Brian Karas.—First edition.
pages   cm
Summary: "On the farm, workers pick vegetables, collect eggs, and make cheese. At the market the next day, the workers set up their stands and prepare for shoppers to arrive. Amy, the baker at the Busy Bee Café, has a very special meal in mind—and, of course, all the farmers show up at the café to enjoy the results of their hard work"—Provided by publisher.
ISBN 978-0-8050-9372-8 (hardback)
[1. Farms—Fiction. 2. Farmers' markets—Fiction.] I. Title.
PZ7.K12960n 2016   [E]—dc23   2015003261

Our books may be purchased in bulk for promotional, educational, or business use.
Please contact your local bookseller or the Macmillan Corporate and Premium Sales Department
at (800) 221-7945 ext. 5442 or by e-mail at MacmillanSpecialMarkets@macmillan.com.

First Edition—2016 / Designed by April Ward
The illustrations for this book were created using gouache and acrylic with pencil on Arches paper.

Printed in China by Toppan Leefung Printing Ltd., Dongguan City, Guangdong Province
1 3 5 7 9 10 8 6 4 2

ON THE
FARM

It's late afternoon and business as usual at the Monterosa Vegetable Farm. Time to get ready for the farmers' market tomorrow morning.

Leo tells his workers which vegetables to pick first. Some vegetables are packed up tonight, while others will be picked early tomorrow. The workers know that greens are best picked soon after the sun rises, when temperatures are still cool.

The vegetables get washed right
away to take out the field's heat.

Empty crates are stacked,
ready for tomorrow's crops.

Then they're packed up
and loaded into trucks.

Soon, everyone but Leo has gone home. He checks to make sure nothing is forgotten.

He snaps a bean
in half and tastes it.
"Perfect," he says.

O ver at the Amazing Cheese Dairy Farm, Isaac is training his new worker, Rachael. He hands her a clipboard. "These are the directions for making cheese," he tells her.

"Remember to put a check mark after you finish each step. And very important—don't miss any steps."

Isaac takes Rachael over to the big steel vat. "To make curds," he explains, "milk goes into this vat. You turn on the heater and stir and stir— and keep on stirring." He shows her how.

Rachael takes the large paddle and stirs like she's rowing a boat in a race. "Not so fast!" says Isaac with a grin.

Rachael stirs until the whey—the liquid—separates from the curds—the chunks.

Next, the curds are scooped up and put into molds, where they become cheese.

The cheeses are placed on racks and allowed to age, some for days and others for months.

Ronnie and Luisa are going over the list of cheeses to be packed into the van early tomorrow morning.

Mozzarella?   Queso Blanco?   Cheddar?

Check.   Yup.   Got it.

Rachael looks at her list to make sure every step has a check mark. "All done!" she reports. "Not yet," says Isaac. He hands her a mop. It's going to be a late night for everybody at the Amazing Cheese Dairy Farm.

Here on Gary's farm, the mushrooms grow in a room on shelves and on bags that hang from the ceiling.

"It resembles a forest, if you think about it," Gary explains. "The plastic bags, filled with a mixture of hay, sawdust, and water, are like tree trunks. Other mushrooms grow on 'cakes' that rest on shelves, like damp logs on the forest floor."

The temperature is cool, and a fog machine keeps the air misty.

Gary trims the mushrooms with sharp scissors
and packs them into foam crates for tomorrow.

It's late and time for sleep, but there's one more job to do. Morning will come too soon.

AT THE
MARKET

Early Sunday, the market gets off to a slow start. The spaces are taken one by one. Nobody talks as tents and tables go up.

A breeze blows, and the tents fill like balloons.
"Wind!" someone yells.
"Tie that corner down! Hold it tight!"

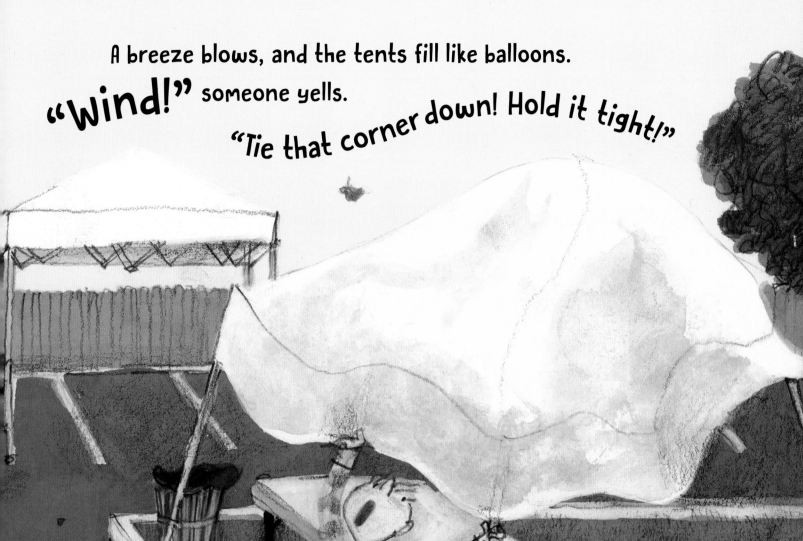

The wind whooshes through,
and it's quiet again.

Sharon, the market manager, comes by with
a tray of steaming cups.
"Who wants hot chocolate?"

Everyone!

Friends catch up with one another.

At 10:00 a.m., customers and browsers start to arrive.

Amy, from the Busy Bee Café, is always one of the first shoppers. She checks in with her favorite farmers.

"What do you have for me today, Leo?"
"Some nice Swiss chard, leeks, and take a look at these tomatoes!" he says, showing them off.

Amy fills her cart. "Perfect for tonight's special," she says as she walks away.

"Save me a table," calls Leo as he weighs broccoli rabe for his next customer.

There are long lines of people. Produce gets weighed, bags get filled, and pies get boxed. Parents carry babies, and kids eat farm-fresh ice cream and cookies.

The Blackberry Hill Fiddlers finally arrive. They unpack,
set up, and soon fill the air with their music.

Next stop for Amy is the Amazing Cheese Farm stand.
"Cheddar cheese, please," she tells Isaac.

"What's for dinner at the Busy Bee tonight?" Isaac asks.
"One way to find out," Amy says, and winks.

The last stop for Amy
is Gary's Mushrooms.
She buys some of
each kind.

MUSHROOMS
OYSTER
SHITAKE
CHANTE
$

Gary looks at Amy's cart. "Hmmm," he says. "Cheddar cheese, Swiss chard, leeks, and mushrooms. And I see you stopped at Henny's Eggs. I can guess what the Busy Bee's special will be tonight."

"Should I save you a seat?" Amy asks him.

"You bet," Gary says.

By the end of the afternoon, the crowd starts to thin out.
Farmers put away what little food is left, and tents come down.

One by one the spaces empty, and soon the only people left are workers cleaning up.

The sky begins to get dark, but the
lights are on over at the Busy Bee Café.
A few of the Blackberry Hill Fiddlers show
up and play a song while everyone sits
down for some of Amy's special Market Pie.
After the hard work on the farm and a long
day at the market, everyone is ready for a

good meal and some fun!

AUTHOR'S NOTE

Because farmers' markets start in the morning, a lot of harvesting, washing, and packing happens at the last minute—some fruits and vegetables can be packed the night before, but others must be picked early in the morning on market day.

Even though much of the work is done at the last possible moment to ensure freshness, growing fruits and vegetables and making cheese takes a lot of work over a long period of time. And for farmers, timing is everything. Knowing when to plant crops and when to pick them, or how long to age a cheese, is part of a farmer's job.

Farmers must take many steps to offer food at its absolute freshest. Anyone who thinks farming is a simple job should talk to a farmer—and then say "thank you"!